EVERYDAY INVENTIONS

INSPIRED BY NATURE

by Samantha S. Bell

FOCUS READERS

FOCUS READERS

WWW.FOCUSREADERS.COM

Focus Readers is distributed by North Star Editions:
sales@northstareditions.com | 888-417-0195

Produced for Focus Readers by Red Line Editorial.

Content Consultant: Ximin He, PhD, Assistant Professor of Materials Science and Engineering, University of California, Los Angeles

Photographs ©: okeyphotos/iStockphoto, cover, 1; Elnur/Shutterstock Images, 4–5; LuckyBusiness/iStockphoto, 7; StephanHoerold/iStockphoto, 8; RamilF/iStockphoto, 10–11; kororokerokero/iStockphoto, 13; Milos-Muller/iStockphoto, 15; XiXinXing/iStockphoto, 16–17; kay roxby/Shutterstock Images, 18–19; Dmitry Grigoriev/Shutterstock Images, 21; Red Line Editorial, 23; unkas_photo/iStockphoto, 24–25; zimowa/Shutterstock Images, 27; Rawpixel/iStockphoto, 29

ISBN
978-1-63517-941-5 (hardcover)
978-1-64185-043-8 (paperback)
978-1-64185-245-6 (ebook pdf)
978-1-64185-144-2 (hosted ebook)

Library of Congress Control Number: 2018932007

Printed in the United States of America
Mankato, MN
May, 2018

ABOUT THE AUTHOR

Samantha Bell is an author/illustrator from South Carolina and has written more than 75 nonfiction books for children. She loves spending time in nature and reading about animals. The more she learns, the more she is amazed at how the natural world works.

TABLE OF CONTENTS

CHAPTER 1

AROUND THE HOUSE

An invention is a new product, process, or way of doing something. Many inventions make certain jobs easier to do. Others help solve specific problems. One way inventors and scientists are solving problems is through biomimicry. In this process, scientists use nature as a guide. First, they observe patterns in nature.

Scientists of biomimicry study plants and animals in their labs.

Then, they create designs that are similar to nature's designs.

Nature has inspired many everyday objects around the house. For example, in 2011, one inventor studied cats' claws to create a safer thumbtack. Regular tacks have sharp pins. They are easy to drop on the floor, where people can step on them.

The pins on the new tacks can be drawn in, similar to the way a cat retracts its claws. In this design, a **sheath** covers the pin. The sheath is made of a rubberlike plastic. The pin stays tucked inside the sheath until pressed into a hard surface.

Other scientists studied the feet of geckos. These small lizards can climb up

Cats extend their claws when they want to use them.

walls. Geckos have stiff **tendons** on their toe pads. These tendons help the gecko grip surfaces. Geckos' toe pads also have millions of tiny hairs. To climb, the gecko places its toe pad on a surface. When it pulls the toe back, the hairs stick to the surface. The hairs unstick when the gecko pulls in a different direction.

Geckos can stick to walls, ceilings, and many other surfaces.

Most **adhesives** are gooey or soft. In 2012, geckos gave scientists a new idea. The scientists created a stiff adhesive. The adhesive is so strong that one small piece can hold up to 700 pounds (318 kg). But it can still be removed easily. The material peels off when pulled upward.

Thanks to cats and geckos, thumbtacks and adhesives are safer and easier to use. Plants and animals are nature's engineers. They are able to adapt and thrive on Earth. They do not harm their environments with waste or pollution. Many scientists believe inventions should work more like the natural world.

STICKING WITH GECKOS

Geckos can cling to wet surfaces. They crawl on wet leaves and branches in their rainy habitats. However, geckos stick best to surfaces that are not completely wet. Their toes create air pockets that keep their feet dry. Scientists hope to make waterproof adhesives based on gecko toes.

CHAPTER 2

HIGH-TECH IMPROVEMENTS

Some nature-inspired inventions improve other machines or products. These are called innovations. For example, many people no longer use **incandescent** light bulbs. Instead, they use LEDs, or light-emitting diodes. These light bulbs use less energy than older bulbs. They also last much longer.

LEDs (top) are less harmful to the environment than incandescent bulbs (bottom).

The first LED light bulbs did not give off enough light. Some of the light was trapped inside the bulbs. Scientists looked to fireflies for an answer. They studied the firefly's light organ. This part of the firefly's body gives off light.

The scientists discovered that the light organ is covered in scales. They also found that the scales do not fit together. Instead, the scales look like shingles on a roof. The sharp edges of the scales cause light rays to scatter. This makes the light look brighter. In 2013, scientists added a similar surface to LED light bulbs. The new surface made the light bulbs 55 percent brighter.

Fireflies glow because of a chemical reaction in their light organs.

Scientists also studied the morpho butterfly's wings. Morpho wings have tiny plates that reflect light. Ridges on the plates form specific patterns. They give the wings a shimmery blue color. In 2009, scientists used a similar design to create a new e-reader. Other e-readers create their own light. But the new e-reader reflects the light around it.

It has tiny mirrors under its screen. The mirrors move in **microseconds**. Similar to morpho wings, the mirrors make patterns to create color images. Reflecting light uses less energy than creating new light. It also makes the screen easier to see in bright light.

Butterflies have also inspired other inventions. One species, called the common rose butterfly, has black wings. Its wings have scales with tiny holes. The holes scatter the sunlight that hits them. That way, the wings can absorb more of the sun's heat. The holes also make the wings lighter. In 2017, scientists used a similar method to help solar panels

New solar panels can absorb light even as the sun sets.

absorb more light. They created panels with tiny holes. Usually, solar panels must be pointed directly at the sun. But the tiny holes could catch light at an angle. This allowed the panels to absorb more light during daylight hours. As a result, they produced more power. The holes also made the panels lighter.

ECHOLOCATION

Many people who are blind use a cane to get around. One scientist is studying bats to make a new type of cane. Bats use a process called echolocation to navigate in the dark. As a bat flies, it makes sounds through its mouth and nose. When the sound waves hit objects, they create echoes. The bat uses the echoes to create a map of its surroundings.

The new cane will work in a similar way. The cane sends out **ultrasonic** waves. Some of the sound waves will sense large, stationary objects. Other sound waves will sense smaller, fast-moving objects. The waves hit an object and bounce back. Then the cane vibrates. The vibrations tell the person where the objects are.

People who are blind use probing canes to sense objects. Soon, these canes may become more advanced.

CHAPTER 3

BETTER BUILDINGS

Nature could be the key to improving the designs of buildings. For example, the orb-weaver spider spins a complex web. The spider's silk reflects **ultraviolet** light. As a result, birds can see the web. They do not fly into it. In 2006, scientists created a coating that works similarly to a spiderweb. It reflects ultraviolet light.

A new window coating makes buildings safer for birds.

The coating makes windows more visible to birds. That way, the birds do not fly into them. Fewer birds are hurt or killed.

Plants have also helped improve buildings. The lotus plant grows in muddy water. But the plant never looks dirty. It has waxy, waterproof leaves and flowers. These leaves are covered in tiny bumps and hairs. When it rains, the small bumps help the rain wash dirt off the plant.

In 2005, scientists came up with a lotus-inspired design for self-cleaning paint. The paint creates a bumpy surface on the wall of the building, similar to the lotus flower. When it rains, the water pushes away dirt, keeping the wall clean.

The Venus flower basket draws in organisms through its mesh walls.

Some buildings even get their shape from nature. The Gherkin is a tower in London, England. It was completed in 2003. The Gherkin's architects were inspired by the Venus flower basket. This tube-shaped sea sponge has a **lattice**-like structure. The mesh pattern makes the sponge very strong.

The Gherkin's outer walls use a similar pattern. This design helps make the building strong. It also creates a natural **ventilation** system. The tower's curved walls allow more air to flow faster around it. Large vents at the bottom suck in the air and move it upward. This helps

KEEPING COOL

Termite mounds maintain a constant temperature. Their shape helps with this process. Cool air comes in at the base of the mound. It moves upward into the mound's warmer areas. Scientists designed a similar system for the Eastgate Centre. This shopping center and office complex is in Harare, Zimbabwe. It uses only one-tenth of the energy needed to cool other buildings of the same size.

the building stay cool, requiring less air conditioning.

DESIGNED BY NATURE

Standard "block" skyscrapers (left) disrupt the flow of wind. The structure of the Gherkin (right) allows for smooth, easy airflow.

CHAPTER 4

FOR THE FUTURE

Scientists and inventors continue to find new ideas. For example, engineers are creating new types of materials for buildings. Today, most buildings are made of concrete and steel. These materials must be made at a very high temperature and pressure. This takes a lot of energy. It also produces carbon dioxide emissions.

Building construction makes up 30 percent of energy use in the United States.

An emission is a release of gas into the space around Earth. High carbon dioxide emissions are harmful to the planet.

New types of building materials could be better for Earth. One engineer is studying bones and eggshells. Bones are made from minerals and proteins.

UP TO THE CHALLENGE

Every year, the Biomimicry Institute in Missoula, Montana, hosts a design challenge. To enter, students form a team of up to eight people. The teams look to nature to solve a global problem. The winning teams earn cash prizes. They also receive free training for creating and selling their products. The Institute hopes the challenge will lead to more nature-inspired inventions.

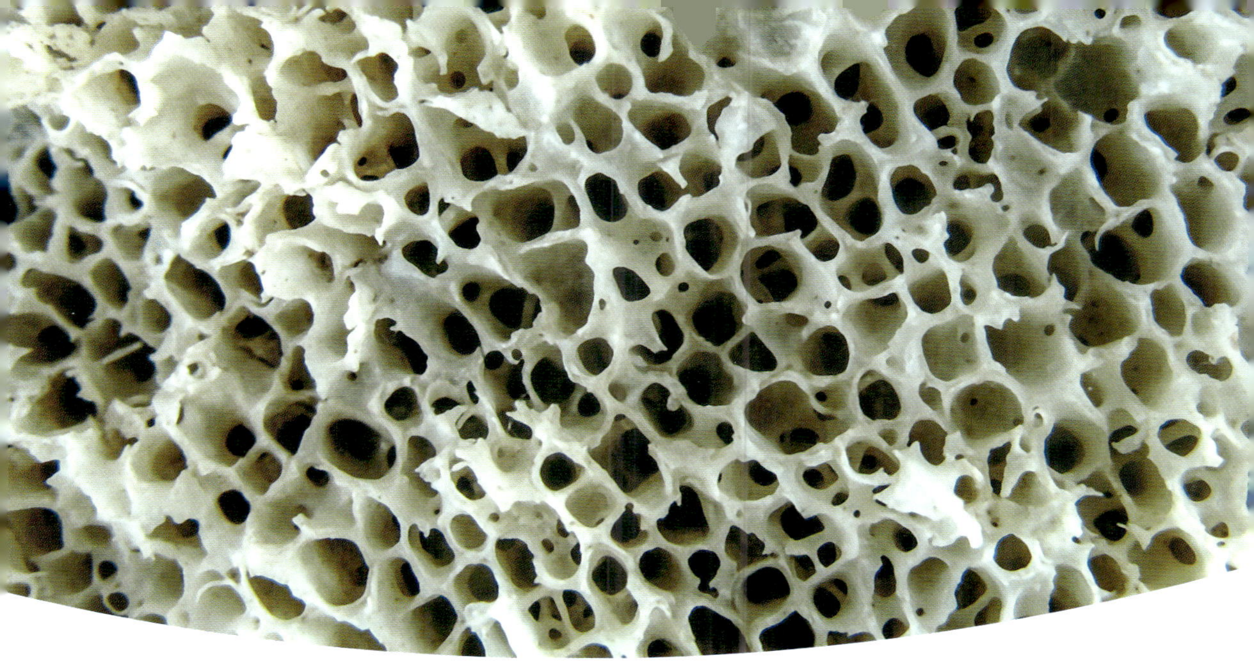

Due to its structure, bone is as strong as cast iron and as light as wood.

Minerals make the bones stiff and hard. Proteins make them strong. Eggshells are also made of minerals. Even though eggshells are very thin, they are strong. The engineer created small samples of artificial bone and eggshells. She made the samples at room temperature. They did not take much energy to produce.

One day, these materials could be used to construct buildings.

A company called Encycle is working on a nature-inspired home improvement. Scientists at the company studied the way bees communicate. In a swarm of bees, each bee helps the entire colony. But the bees don't need instruction from the queen bee. They automatically work together.

Scientists are using this information to help manage energy in homes. Home appliances usually work independently. The new energy system allows appliances to share information. This way, they can spread out the demand for energy. Each

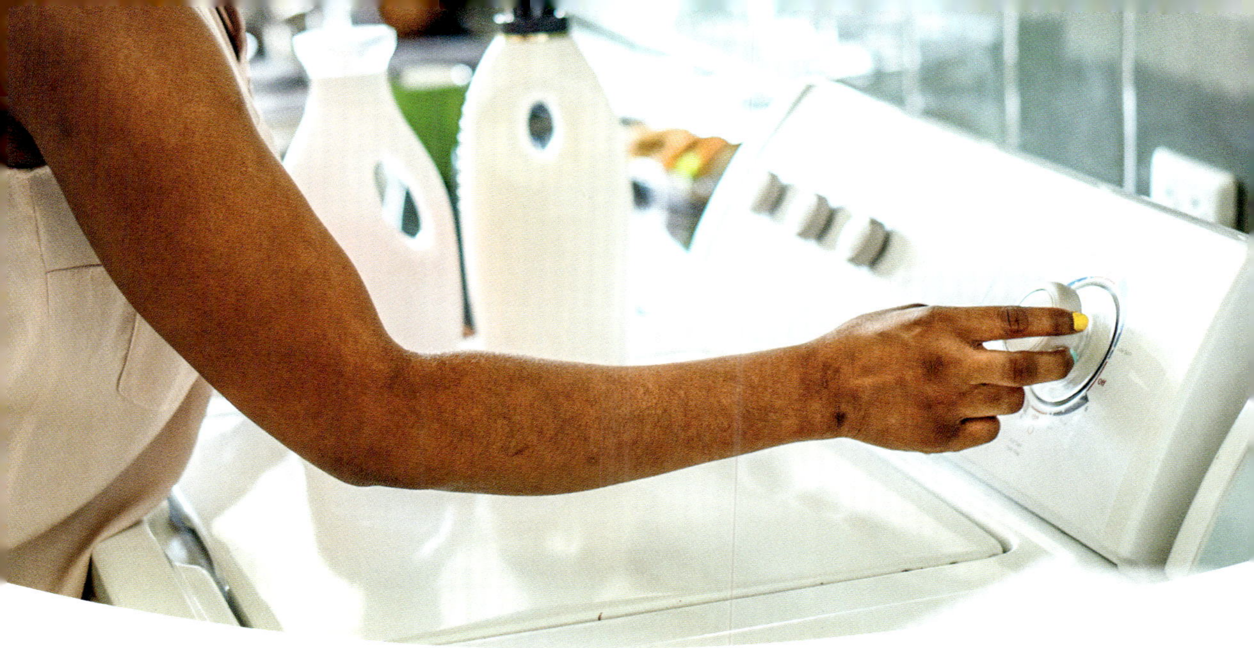

Nearly 35 percent of energy use in US homes goes toward appliances, electronics, and lighting.

appliance turns on and off based on the demand of the other appliances. This could lower buildings' electric bills.

These inventions are not yet finished. But they could have long-lasting effects. By looking to nature, scientists find new answers to old problems. Their inventions can make everyday life easier and safer.

FOCUS ON

EVERYDAY INVENTIONS INSPIRED BY NATURE

Write your answers on a separate piece of paper.

1. Write a paragraph that summarizes how scientists created one of the inventions in Chapter 1.

2. Which nature-inspired invention would you want to own? Why?

3. Which invention was inspired by a butterfly?

   A. a new type of solar panel
   B. LED light bulbs
   C. self-cleaning paint

4. What would be one benefit of using artificial bones and eggshells as building materials?

   A. Construction of buildings would take less time.
   B. They are better for the environment than concrete and steel.
   C. They allow more natural light into the buildings.

Answer key on page 32.

GLOSSARY

adhesives
Substances used for sticking objects together.

incandescent
A type of light bulb that gives off light when heated.

lattice
A structure made of strips that cross one another.

microseconds
Units that are one-millionth of a second.

sheath
A close-fitting cover, often for something sharp.

tendons
Tissues in the body that attach muscles to bones.

ultrasonic
Having to do with sounds that are too high for humans to hear.

ultraviolet
Light that is invisible to human eyes and has a shorter wavelength than that of visible light.

ventilation
The process of allowing fresh air to enter and move through a room or building.

TO LEARN MORE

BOOKS

Gregory, Josh. *From Butterfly Wings to . . . Display Technology*. Ann Arbor, MI: Cherry Lake Publishing, 2014.

Verstraete, Larry. *Innovations in Everyday Technologies*. New York: Crabtree Publishing, 2017.

Yomtov, Nel. *From Termite Den to . . . Office Building*. Ann Arbor, MI: Cherry Lake Publishing, 2014.

NOTE TO EDUCATORS

Visit **www.focusreaders.com** to find lesson plans, activities, links, and other resources related to this title.

INDEX

Answer Key: 1. Answers will vary; **2.** Answers will vary; **3.** A; **4.** B